KU-386-047

Schools Library and Information Services
S00000733255

First published in 2003 by Uitgeverij Clavis, Amsterdam - Hasselt
First dual language publication in 2004 by Mantra Lingua

A CIP record for this book is available from the British Library.

Published by Mantra Lingua
5 Alexandra Grove, London N12 8NU
www.mantralingua.com

آصدقاء فلوپي
Floppy's Friends

Guido van Genechten

Arabic translation by Dr Sajida Fawzi

mantra

يخرج فلوپي كل يوم بعد
المدرسة ليلعب مع أصدقائه.
وكان أصدقاء فلوپي من كل الالوان
والاحجام ولكن...

Every day, after school,
Floppy went out to play
with his friends.
Floppy's friends were all
sizes and colours but…

هم يلعبون فقط مع
الأرانب التي تشبههم.

they only ever played with the
rabbits who looked like them.

" أتمنى لو كُنا نستطيع أن نلعب معاً،"
فكّر فلوپي.

“I wish we could all play together,”
thought Floppy.

وجرى فلوپي ليلعب أوّلا لعبة
لا – تسقط – الجزرة مع الأرانب البيضاء.

First Floppy ran to play don’t-drop-the-carrot
with the white rabbits.

ولم يُسقط فلوپي الجزرة أبدا حتى
عندما وثب على ساق واحدة.

Floppy didn’t drop the carrot once,
not even when he hopped on one leg.

وبعد ذلك لعب فلوپي لعبة طيّر – طيّارة مع الأرانب الرمادية.
" أعلى، أعلى وحلّق!" ردّد فلوپي. " ولكن احذر موضع نزولك."

Next Floppy played fly-a-kite with the grey rabbits.
“Up, up and away!” chanted Floppy. “But watch your landing.”

ثم لعب فلوپي لعبة قفزة الضفدع مع الأرانب البنيّة.
" اقفز أعلى واقفز من فوق!" ردّد فلوپي.

Then Floppy played leapfrog with the brown rabbits.
"Jump up and jump over!" chanted Floppy.

وأخيرا لعب فلوپي لعبة القطار مع الأرانب السوداء.
" هل من الممكن أن أكون السائق؟" سأل فلوپي.
" حسناً،" قالت الأرانب السوداء.
تذكروا آخر مرة عندما كان فلوپي في
وسط القطار وسبّب أكبر اصطدام!

Finally Floppy played trains with the black rabbits.
"Can I be the driver?" asked Floppy.
"Ok," said the black rabbits. They remembered the last time Floppy
was in the middle of the train, he caused the most enormous crash!

وفي عصر اليوم التالي كان هناك أرنب صغير وحيد واقفاً تحت الشجرة.
لم يكن أبيضاً ولم يكن رمادياً. لم يكن بنّياً ولم يكن أسوداً.
كان مرقطاً باللون البنّي والأبيض.
كان يراقب كل الأرانب تلعب وتمرح وتمنّى لو يستطيع مشاركتهم.
ولكنه كان جديداً ولم يكن يعرف أحداً ولم يعرف ألعابهم.

The next afternoon under a tree stood a lonely little rabbit.
He wasn't white and he wasn't grey. He wasn't brown and
he wasn't black. He was dappled brown and white.
He watched all the rabbits having fun and wished that he could join in.
But being new he didn't know anybody and he didn't know their games.

عندما رأى فلوپي الأرنب الجديد ذهب إليه
وتحدّث معه. " أهلاً، أنا فلوپي.
ما اسمكَ؟" سأله فلوپي.
" سامي،" قال الأرنب المرقّط.
" تعال والعب،" قال فلوپي.
" ولكن لا أعرف كيف ألعب ألعابكم،" قال سامي.
" لا تهتم. أنا سأريك ذلك،" قال فلوپي.

When Floppy saw the new rabbit he
went over to him. “Hi, I’m Floppy.
What’s your name?” he asked.
“Samy,” said the dappled rabbit.
“Come and play,” said Floppy.
“But I don’t know how to play
your games,” said Samy.
“Don’t worry. I’ll show you,”
said Floppy.

قام فلوپي بتعليم سامي لعبة لا – تُسقِط – الجزرة.
وضع فلوپي الجزرة على رأسه ومشى.
" رائع،" قال سامي.

Floppy showed Samy don't-drop-the-carrot.
Floppy put the carrot on his head and off he went.
"Cool," said Samy.

ثُمّ جاء دور سامي. وضع الجزرة على رأسه.
" أنظر، إنه أمر سهل!" قال فلوپي.

Then it was Samy’s turn. He put the carrot on his head.
“See, it’s easy!” said Floppy.

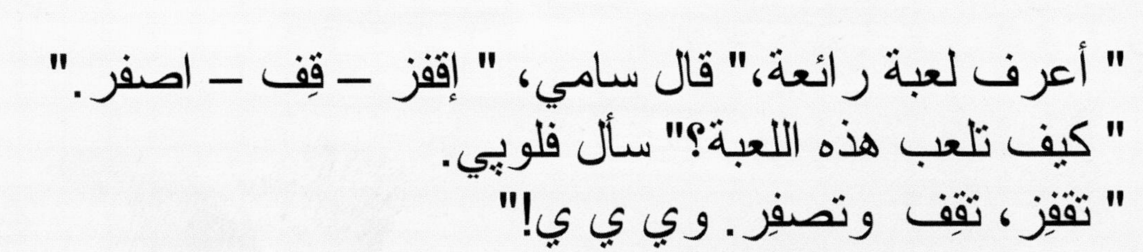

" أعرف لعبة رائعة،" قال سامي، " إقفز – قِف – اصفر."
" كيف تلعب هذه اللعبة؟" سأل فلوپي.
" تقفِز، تقِف وتصفِر. وي ي ي!"
" رائع!" ضحك فلوپي.

"I know a really cool game,"
said Samy, "skip-stop-whistle."
"How d'you play that?"
asked Floppy.
"You skip, stop and whistle:
WHEEEE!"
"Cool!" laughed Floppy.

وجاءت الأرانب الأخرى لِترى ماذا يجري.
" هذا سامي،" قال فلوپي.
" سامي،" قَهقَهَ أرنب كبير،
" يجب أن يُسمّى أبقع."
وضحك الجميع،
كلهم ماعدا فلوپي وسامي.

The other rabbits came to see what was going on.
“This is Samy,” said Floppy.
“Samy,” giggled a big rabbit. “He should be called Spotty.”
They all laughed, all except Floppy and Samy.

" أبقع! أبقع! سا – مي أب – قع!" ردّدت الأرانب الأخرى.

“Spotty! Spotty! Sa-my is spo-tty!”
the other rabbits chanted.

" كفى!" صاح فلوپي.
" يعرف سامي لعبة رائعة حقاً."
" أصحيح هذا! ما هي؟"

"Stop it!" shouted Floppy.
"Samy knows a really cool game."
"Oh yeah! What's that?"

" طيّر جزرة – طيّارة – قفزة الضفدع – في – ال – قطار
مع اقفِز، قِف واصفر."
" كيف تلعب ذلك إذاً؟" سأل الأرنب الكبير.

"Fly-a-carrot-kite-leapfrog-on-the-train
with a skip, stop and whistle."
"How d'you play that then?"
asked the big rabbit.

" حسناً،" قال فلوپي. " تضع جزرة على رأسك،
تطيّر طيّارة، قفزة الضفدع – في – ال – قطار،
اقفِز، قِف واصفر، وي ي ي!"
وشاركت كل الأرانب في لعبة سامي الرائعة.

“Well,” said Floppy. “You put a carrot on your
head, fly-a-kite, leapfrog-on-the-train,
skip, stop and whistle: WHEEEE!”
All the rabbits joined in
Samy’s cool game.

ولعب كل أصدقاء فلوپي معاً.

And ALL Floppy's friends played together!